# Old King Cole
and friends

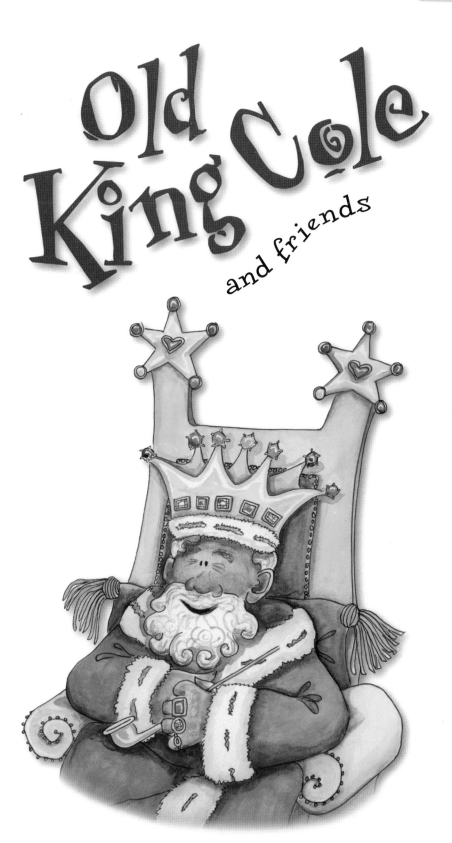

Miles Kelly

First published in 2011 by Miles Kelly Publishing Ltd
Harding's Barn, Bardfield End Green, Thaxted, Essex, CM6 3PX, UK

2 4 6 8 10 9 7 5 3 1

**Editorial Director** Belinda Gallagher

**Art Director** Jo Cowan

**Editor** Sarah Parkin

**Cover/Junior Designer** Kayleigh Allen

**Production Manager** Elizabeth Collins

**Reprographics** Stephan Davis, Ian Paulyn

ISBN 978-1-84810-414-3

Printed in China

British Library Cataloguing-in-Publication Data
A catalogue record for this book is available from the British Library

**ACKNOWLEDGEMENTS**

Artworks are from the Miles Kelly Artwork Bank
Cover artist: Kirsten Wilson

Made with paper from a sustainable forest

www.mileskelly.net
info@mileskelly.net

www.factsforprojects.com

Self-publish your
children's book

buddingpress.co.uk

# Contents

# This is the Way

This is the way the ladies ride,
Tri, tre, tre, tree, tri, tre, tre, tree;
This is the way the ladies ride,
Tri, tre, tre, tre, tri-tre-tre-tree!

*Pretend to be a lady gently riding a horse. Next pretend to be a gentleman galloping along. Then pretend to be a farmer hobbling along.*

This is the way the gentlemen ride,
Gallop-a-trip, gallop-a-trot;
This is the way the gentlemen ride,
Gallop-a-gallop-a-trot!

This is the way the farmers ride,
Hobbledy-hoy, hobbledy-hoy;
This is the way the farmers ride,
Hobbledy, hobbledy-hoy!

# Where, O Where

Where, O where,
Has my little dog gone?
O where, O where, can he be?
With his tail cut short,
And his ears cut long,
O where, O where, has he gone?

# Mary's Lamb

Mary had a little lamb,
Its fleece was white as snow;
And everywhere that Mary went
The lamb was sure to go.

It followed her to school one day,
That was against the rules.
It made the children laugh and play,
To see a lamb at school.

# Ding, Dong Bell

Ding, dong bell,
Pussy's in the well.

Who put her in?
Little Johnny Green.

Who pulled her out?
Little Johnny Stout.

What a naughty boy was that
To try to drown poor pussy cat,

Who never did him any harm,
But killed the mice in his father's barn.

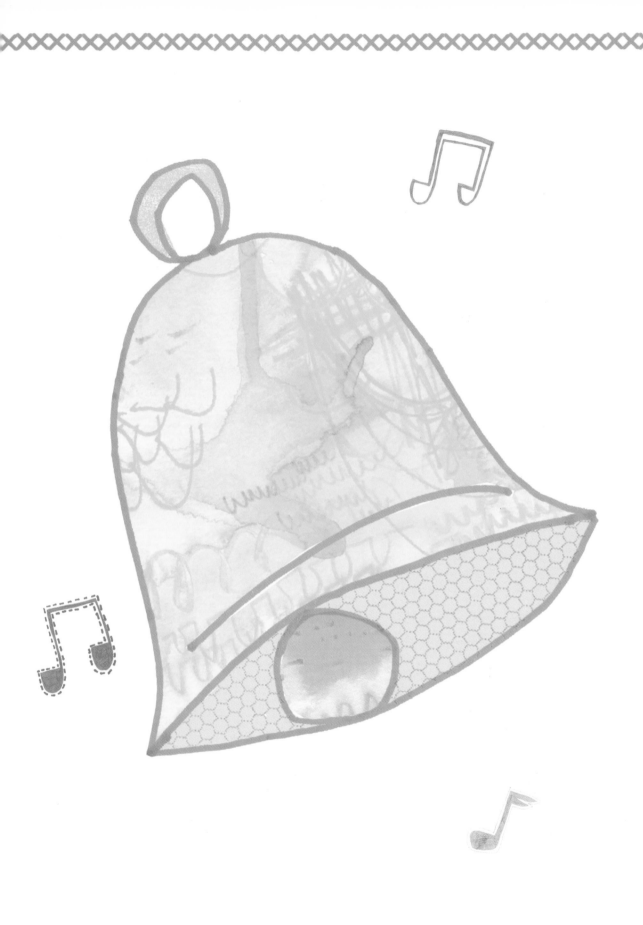

# Jack and the Beanstalk

A retelling from the original tale
by Joseph Jacobs

Jack and his mother were very poor and there came a sad day when there was no more money left, so Jack was told to take the cow to market to sell her.

As Jack led the cow to market, he met a little man with a tall feather in his hat.

"Where might you be going with that fine-looking cow?" the little man asked.

Jack explained and the little man swept

off his hat with the tall feather, and shook out five coloured beans.

"Well, young Jack, I will give you these magic beans in exchange for your cow."

Now Jack should have realized that this was all rather odd, for how did the little man know his name? But once he heard the word 'magic' he didn't stop to think. He took the beans at once, gave the little man the cow and ran off home to his mother.

"Jack, you are a complete fool! You have exchanged our fine cow for five worthless beans!" She flung the beans out of the window, and sent Jack to bed without any supper.

When he woke in the morning, Jack couldn't understand why it was so dark in the cottage. He rushed outside to find his mother staring at the most enormous beanstalk that reached up into the clouds.

"I told you they were magic beans," smiled Jack, and he began to climb the beanstalk. He climbed until he could no longer see the ground. When he reached the top there stood a castle. Jack knocked at the door, and it was opened by a huge woman!

"My husband eats little boys for breakfast so you better run away quickly," she said to Jack. But before Jack could reply, the ground started to shake and tremble.

"Too late!" said the giant's wife. "You must hide," and she bundled Jack into a cupboard. Jack peeped through the keyhole, and saw the most colossal man. "Fee fi fo fum! I smell the blood of an Englishman!"

"Don't be silly, dear. You can smell the sausages I have just cooked for your breakfast," said the giant's wife, placing a plate piled high with fat, juicy sausages in front of him. The giant did not seem to have very good table manners, and had soon gobbled the lot. Then he poured a great bag of gold onto the table, and counted all the coins. With a smile on his big face, he soon fell asleep.

Jack darted out of the cupboard, grabbed the bag of money and ran out of the kitchen. He slithered down the beanstalk as fast as he could and there, standing at the bottom, was his mother. She was amazed when she saw the gold.

Jack's mother bought two new cows and she and Jack were very content now they had plenty to eat. But after a while Jack decided he would like to climb the beanstalk again. The giant's wife was not pleased to see him.

"My husband lost a bag of gold the last time you were here," she muttered looking closely at Jack. But then the ground began to shake and tremble. Jack hid in the cupboard again.

The giant stomped into the kitchen.

"Fee fi fo fum! I smell the blood of an Englishman!" he roared.

"Don't be silly, dear. You can smell the chickens I have just cooked for your breakfast," said the giant's wife, placing a plate piled high with thirty-eight chickens in front of him. The giant had soon gobbled the lot. Then he lifted a golden hen onto the table, and said, "Lay!" and the hen laid a golden egg. With a smile on his big face he fell asleep, snoring loudly.

Jack darted out of the cupboard, grabbed the golden hen and ran out of the kitchen. He slithered down the beanstalk as fast as he could and there, standing at the bottom, was his mother. She was astonished when she saw the hen.

Jack's mother bought a whole herd of cows. She also bought lots of new clothes for herself and Jack, and they were very content. But after a while Jack decided he would like to climb the beanstalk one last time. Again, the giant's wife was not pleased to see him.

"My husband lost a golden hen the last time you were here," and she peered closely at Jack. But then the ground began to shake and tremble. Jack hid under the table.

The giant stomped into the kitchen.

"Fee fi fo fum! I smell the blood of an Englishman!" he roared.

"I would look in the cupboard if I were you," said the giant's wife. But of course the cupboard was empty. They were both puzzled. The giant trusted his nose, and his wife didn't know where Jack had gone.

"Eat your breakfast, dear. I have just cooked you ninety-two fried eggs," said the giant's wife, placing a plate in front of him. The giant had soon gobbled the lot. Then he lifted a golden harp onto the table, and said, "Play!" and the harp played so sweetly that the giant was soon fast asleep.

Jack crept out from under the table and grabbed the golden harp, but as soon as he touched it the harp called out, "Master, master!" and the giant awoke with a great start. He chased after Jack who scrambled down the beanstalk as fast as he could with the harp in his arms. As soon as Jack reached the ground he raced to get a big axe, and chopped through the beanstalk. Down tumbled the great beanstalk, down tumbled the giant and that was the end of them both!

Jack and his mother lived very happily for the rest of their days. The bag of gold never ran out, the hen laid a golden egg every day, and the harp soon forgot about the giant and played sweetly for Jack and his mother.

# The Cow

The friendly cow all red and white,
I love with all my heart;
She gives me cream with all her might,
To eat with apple tart.

She wanders lowing here and there,
And yet she cannot stray,
All in the pleasant open air,
The pleasant light of day.

And blown by all the winds that pass
And wet with all the showers,
She walks among the meadow grass
And eats the meadow flowers.

Robert Louis Stevenson
1850–94, b. Scotland

# As I was going out

As I was going out one day
My head fell off and rolled away.
But when I saw that it was gone,
I picked it up and put it on.

And when I got into the street
A fellow cried, "Look at your feet!"
I looked at them and sadly said,
"I've left them both asleep in bed!"

# Old King Cole

Old King Cole was a merry old soul,
And a merry old soul was he;
He called for his pipe,
And he called for his bowl,
And he called for his fiddlers three.

Every fiddler, he had a fine fiddle,
And a very fine fiddle had he;
Oh, there's none so rare as can compare
With King Cole and his fiddlers three.

# Two Cats of Kilkenny

There once were two cats of Kilkenny,
Each thought there was
One cat too many,
So they fought and they fit,
And they scratched and they bit,
Till, excepting their nails
And the tips of their tails,
Instead of two cats,
there weren't any.

# Bonfire Night

Remember, remember
The fifth of November,
Gunpowder, treason and plot.
I see no reason why gunpowder, treason
Should ever be forgot...

# The Hare and the Tortoise

Retold from the original fable
by Aesop

The day that Tortoise challenged Hare to a race, all the animals laughed so hard that their tummies ached. But Tortoise was fed-up with Hare whizzing round him all the time, teasing him about how slow he was. I'll show that Hare, if it's the last thing I do! Tortoise promised himself.

Hare thought that Tortoise's little joke was extremely funny. For that's all Hare thought it was – a joke. Hare never expected that Tortoise would actually go through with his mad idea. So his eyes nearly popped out of his head when he arrived at the starting line to see Tortoise already there, limbering up in a very slow, stiff, creaky sort of way.

"Be careful there, old chap!" Hare worried, as he realized his friend was serious. "You don't want to do yourself an injury."

"Don't worry about me," replied Tortoise. "You should be working out how you're going to beat me. Ha! You won't see me for dust!"

A crowd of animals had gathered to watch the race and they all cheered and clapped and jumped up and down at Tortoise's bold remark.

Suddenly, Hare started to feel rather annoyed. "All right then. If that's the way you want it!" he snapped. "I was going to give you a headstart, but obviously you won't be wanting one."

"No need," breezed Tortoise, although his little heart was pumping inside his shell. "First one to the windmill's the winner."

Hare peered into the distance. The windmill was three fields away. He could get there in less than a minute without losing his breath. But surely it would take Tortoise all day to reach it!

"Three! Twit-Two! One!" cried Barn Owl, and Tortoise lifted one leg over the starting line amid thunderous applause.

The stunned Hare watched in amazement as Tortoise began to crawl slowly away. 'Well, you have to hand it to Tortoise,' Hare thought, seeing the funny side of things again. 'He's got a good sense of humour and a lot of guts!'

Hare sat down next to the starting line under a shady tree. It was a beautiful sunny day and it was very pleasant to sit there in the dappled light, watching Tortoise amble peacefully into the field.

Hare's eyes shut and his head drooped before he even realized he was sleepy . . .

Meanwhile, Tortoise was remembering what his mum had told him as a child: Slow and steady does it, son. Slow and steady does it. And Tortoise kept on going and didn't give up . . .

Hare didn't wake up until the night air was so cold that it was freezing his whiskers. Where am I? he thought. And then suddenly he remembered the race. Hare leapt to his feet and squinted into the moonlight, but there was no sign of Tortoise. All at once, he heard a faint sound of cheering coming from a long way off, and he saw tiny dark figures jumping up and down around the windmill. "Surely not!" Hare gasped, and shot off over the fields like an arrow. He arrived at the windmill just in time to see all the animals hoisting Tortoise – the champion! – on their shoulders. And of course, after that, Hare never ever teased his friend about being slow again.

# Hush, Little Baby

Hush, little baby, don't say a word,
Papa's going to buy you a mocking bird.

If that mocking bird won't sing,
Papa's going to buy you a diamond ring.

If that diamond ring turns brass,
Papa's going to buy you a looking-glass.

If that looking-glass gets broke,
Papa's going to buy you a billy-goat.

If that billy-goat won't pull,
Papa's going to buy you a cart and bull.

35

# See-saw, Margery Daw

See-saw, Margery Daw,
Johnny shall have a new master;
He shall have but a penny a day,
Because he can't work any faster.

An ideal rhyme for playing in the park.

Or sit on the floor facing your partner holding hands.

Gently rock backwards and forwards as if you were on a see-saw.

# Little Tommy Tucker

Little Tommy Tucker,
Sings for his supper.
What shall we give him?
White bread and butter.
How shall he cut it
Without a knife?
How will he be married
Without a wife?

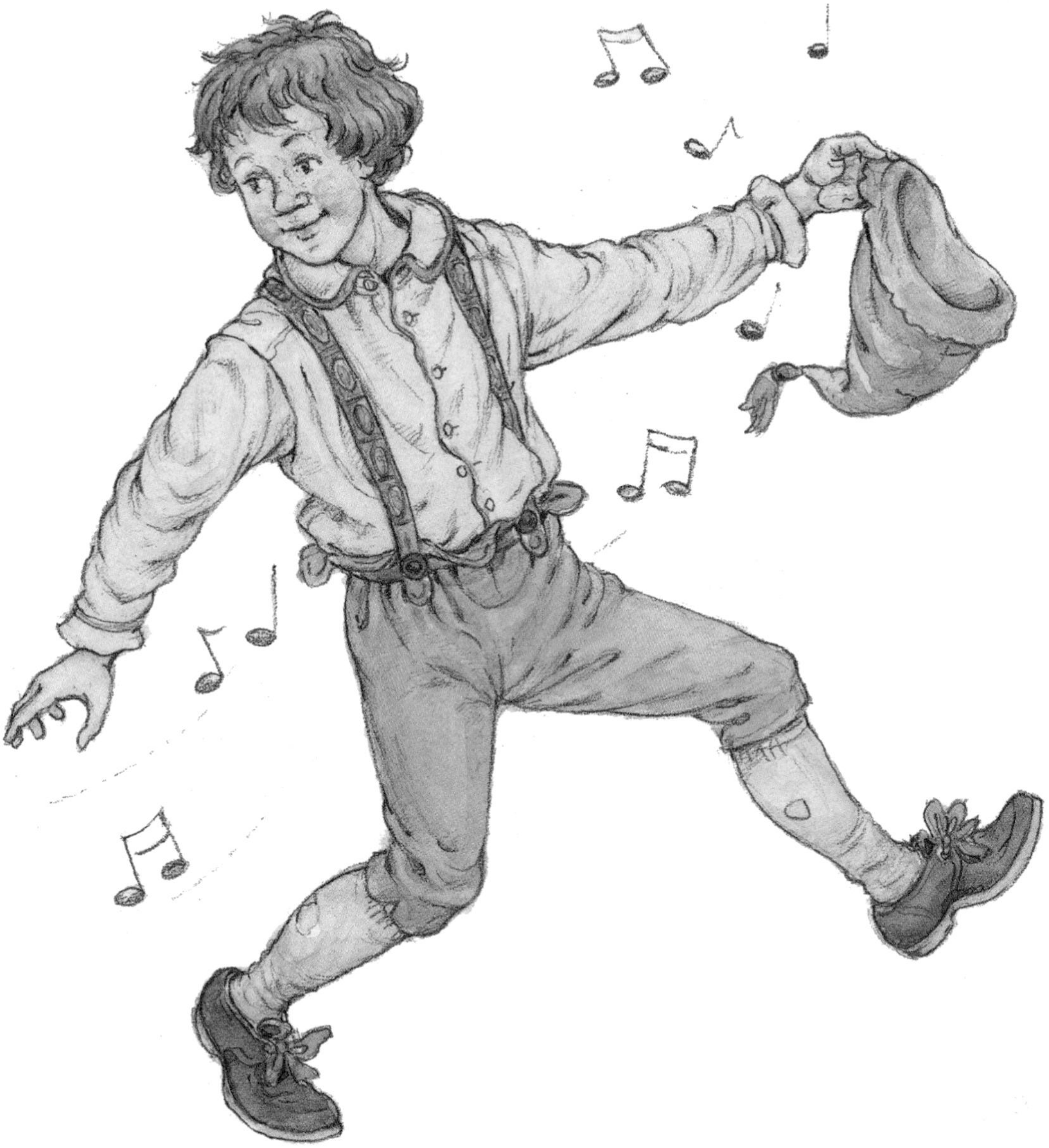

# Rain

The rain is falling all around,
It falls on field and tree,
It rains on the umbrellas here,
And on the ships at sea.

Robert Louis Stevenson
1850–94, b. Scotland

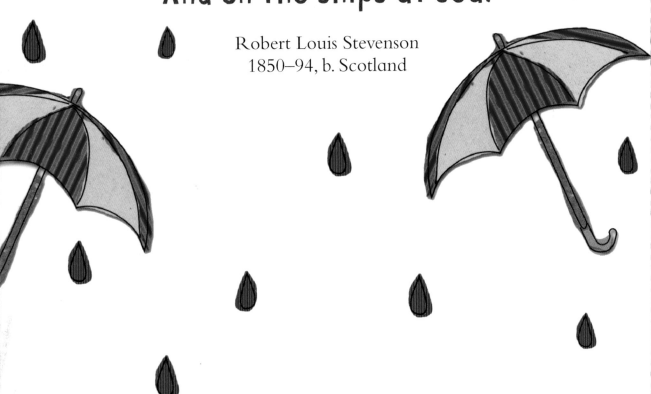